Adv
BECOMII

"The fingerprints of the unflinching poems in Mary Ann Honaker's *Becoming Persephone* will not soon fade away. These poems are rife with gothic power chords and break into all the gender dispensaries, stealing 'boots stirruped by bullets,' 'lopsided sobs,' and the 'smashed glamour' of damned hands. Like the oracular smoke from the crack in the earth at Delphi, the subterranean damage in this book is equal parts intoxicating and terrifying." --Simeon Berry, author of *Ampersand Revisited* and *Monograph*

"'Ye gods it was not meant to be like this.' Mary Ann Honaker's searing narratives show that resisting convention, as a young woman, does not liberate you from men's cruelties. 'You cannot cut time/like a fishing line/let the past drift downstream,' she writes. Still, the book's later poems, redemptive and illuminated, insist that 'This body is not a coffin.' In this moving journey, we experience the descent, but we return to the world and its sensual affirmations. This is a book that needed to be written. It needs to be read." – J.D. Scrimgeour, author of *Lifting the Turtle*

"*Becoming Persephone* is an accomplished debut of raw narratives which confront drug and alcohol use, teenage angst, violence, and rape. Throughout this collection, Honaker doesn't look away but rather into these experiences. These poems do what all excellent writing seeks to do; they find words for 'the nighttime pouring out' of us. It is because Honaker authenticates this dark quotidian that she is also able to transcend it. Honaker prepares us all 'To sit on the lip of a rowboat/ and dry out what's needed/for flight.'" --Eileen Cleary, author of *Child Ward of the Commonwealth*

"The stakes are high in *Becoming Persephone*, a harrowing poetic trip through the treacherous shoals of contemporary adult America. But Honaker's words have the buoyancy and the nimbleness to navigate the reader through this stunning, violent journey."--Tim Peeler, author of *West of Mercy* and *Checking Out*

Other books by Mary Ann Honaker

It Will Happen Like This   978-1548480196

BECOMING
PERSEPHONE

Mary Ann Honaker

Mary Honaker

Third Lung
Press

2019

Third Lung Press
3452 50th Ave Cir NE
Hickory NC 28601
newthirdlungpress@gmail.com

ISBN 978-0-578-22521-0

Cover Photograph by Nordwood from *Unsplash*

"We go through a Plutonian time, where we go down into the depths of things and draw out the dregs so that they can be made holy again... We go back, take a journey back in time, to retrieve a part of ourselves."

--Aepril Schaile, Nuit Report 4-27-18
aeprilsarcana.com

"You'll never untangle the circumstances that brought you to this moment. You're a warrior. Arise now, mighty warrior."

– the Bhagavad Gita

Table of Contents

I

II

III

Acknowledgments

Thank you to the editors of the journals in which these poems have appeared:

805 Art + Lit. "Fog on Derby Wharf"

Coe Review. "Becoming Persephone," and "Nothing But the Blood"

Drunk Monkeys. "Below Zero, with Wind Chill," "Feral,""Poem with a Stolen Line" and "Tomboy"

Every Pigeon. "Tuesday is Trash Day"

Figure 1. "Divorcing Plato"

Indolent Books' *What Rough Beast Series.* "Pierced Septum"

The Lake. "Two-Bird Hymn to Ishtar"

Lily Poetry Review. "The Light Chain"

The Literary Nest. "Turn Lane"

Topology. "Jazz Birds"

Transcendence Magazine. "Threshold"

For every woman who has spoken out

and every woman who remains silent

I

I was joyfully gathering flowers,

when the earth beneath me gave way.

--from "Homeric Hymn to Demeter"
trans. by Gregory Nagy

The Pledge

I lost my first dog when I was five:
a hyper little terrier mix
adopted from the pound.

He simply disappeared.
I remember crying over Cheerios
one morning before kindergarten.

We didn't know
this was only the beginning.

§

Someone in the neighborhood
was killing the dogs.
The children's dogs.

The girl across the road from me
found her small wiry white dog
with an oily tire track

across its uncrushed body,
tongue lolled out, covered
in grit, the scene looking staged.

My cousins' dog outside
our driveway, my mom's
wing-like hands over my eyes,

over my brother's eyes.
We stood behind kitchen curtains
listening to our cousins wail,

my mother murmuring
you can't look, there's too much
blood, gathering us against her sides.

§

We all felt certain we knew
the culprit, but my dad said,
You can't go accusing

someone without evidence.
This is how I learned
even adults are helpless

in a world cruel and unjust.

§

A St. Bernard, my uncle's
wrinkly old smiling mutt,
the Pritchard's mid-size yapper

one by one, vanished,
collapsed, having been poisoned,
or found by the roadside:

one by my brother and I
with blood spindling
from his open mouth--

and we, two children,
broke the news to the mother.
Her face suddenly blank

as a shaken Etch A Sketch.
She thanked us, shut the door.
We trudged home, kicking gravel,

while a chorus of shouts, weeping
trailed us like accusers.

Scruffy. Muffin. Ethel. Hattie.
Deputy. King. Sargent. Fluffy.

Does it help to say
their names, a childhood's
unending eulogy?

§

On the forest path, spangled
with a confetti of shade & sun,
my friend Heather's uncle found

my black collie, fur tacky with blood,
her eyes as blank as sun-smashed windows.
The uncle told my dad who took a shovel

into secret shade and dug a grave.
This is what she said to me in the front yard,
beside the bush glittered with ruby-red

poisonous berries, on the shorn lawn,
where of course such a thing was impossible.
She'd gotten lost and was even now,

nose to the ground, hobbling on
her three legs home, thinking of me;
she'd found a rainwater puddle,

she'd slaked her thirst, she would stagger
into the shade of the trees tomorrow,
at the latest. I yelled at my friend--

NO, YOU'RE LYING while her eyes ebbed
on a shoreline I couldn't then reach.
A small closet in my mind opened,

hung her unseasonal coat of words, shut.
This was when I made the pledge
to never again love too much.

The Experiment

I left the guy I lost my virginity to
because he always wanted to be together,
and I was growing bored

of shoplifting sprees at the mall,
sneaking food into movies, the smell
of his cigarettes-- Montclairs,

which produced a thick and sour smoke,
insistently strong, that clung to me, my clothes,
the way he clung to me, calling as soon as

I'd left his house, wanting to talk until
I fell asleep, phone in my hand.
I just couldn't take him anymore.

A woman should have more feeling
for the guy she lost it to, they said,
someone said, maybe someone in my mind.

I was amazed at how well I knew
little things about him: how his wallet
became as singular to me as a fingerprint,

how familiar I'd grown with the rectangular
crease it made in the back pocket of his jeans,
every key on his key ring. But it

didn't add up to love, nothing ever did.
She's cold, they said, or I thought they said,
She's slutty, they definitely said, no guess needed.

§

A woman should have more feeling,
should write love letters and cry.
A woman should take a break-up hard.

A woman should have more feeling:
she should hang in and hang in. She should
forgive seven times seventy.

§

So for no particular reason I decided
to hang in. It was a test, an experiment.
Could I love? When he told me,

Once a slut, always a slut, I hung in.
When he was unfaithful, I hung in.
When he raised a hand to me the first time.

When he choked me and his friend
had to pull him off me, drag him
in a strangle-hold to another room.

Maybe I was making a point, to him,
to *them*. Maybe I thought I deserved it,
because I couldn't love him:

a secret balled up and tucked away
where I couldn't find it. I wanted to prove
I could love despite myself, for myself.

Finally one night, he punched me repeatedly
in my right ear. To this day my ear will shiver
with sharp pains and ring when the weather changes

[20]

to cold, cold like I am. I was relieved
when I finally walked away, only relieved.
A real woman would write love poems, grieve.

Feral

It was a time of small beauties:
cigarette ashes flicked from car

windows aglow in staggered rows
like released Japanese lanterns,

bonfires in fields, in pits
dug in the coarse sand by the river,

a lovely thin-waisted boy
pouring beer over scraggly locks,

tossing coal black hair back: an arc
of sun-sparked jewels,

bright beads spilling down
bared chest, a crackling laugh

the final slay. To this day
I'm swifted back to those lean,

hard-drinking years by the scent
of cigarettes overlaying the spicy musk

of still-crisp, newfallen leaves,
the odor like a forgotten but favorite

metallic guitar riff-- I thumb through
the cassette inserts of my mind,

find my mouth forming a feral grin,
my face forgetting twenty years

in twenty seconds. In photos,
I'm all whites of eyes, a timid doe

inclined to flight or a menaced
coyote inclined to bite, seconds

from a toothy snap. We yapped
through the night like dogs, whooped

at the moon encased in a fuzzy aura
of drunken sway. We fucked without shame,

pissed without asking pardon. We woke
to gnawing mornings, groped for soda,

stomachs unsettled and foreheads
filled with lint and cotton ticking.

I wrote of lust and headlights reflected
by roadside puddles, of love

and games of pool. Somehow we knew
it would get harder from here on out,

and took our revenge greedily & soon,
breaking into houses, stealing what

we couldn't buy, cheating each other,
bleeding each other, perfecting pristine lies.

We drank everything we could stomach.
We carried small knives and brass knuckles,

slung back our shoulders, wore heavy boots.
We readied ourselves for the coming fight.

More Love, More Power

In your bedroom you showed us
your stack of juvenile offender
records: a novella of rebellion.

Your ex's picture smiled at us
in jealous supervision. Quietly
we dwelt on her face,

then a shout and a kick:
the photo face down
on the floor, encircled

by glass shards. This
is why I chose him, not you:
I could see myself reflected

in all those glittering pieces,
myself knowing myself partial,
sharp-edged, incomplete,

unable to be as whole to you
as she was. And godammit
wasn't I right?

§

Myself in pieces: my black
and menacing armor shattered.
Just a girl, like any other.

No. I wanted all the power,
wanted you only if I could hold
the breakable glass of you

[24]

in my hand, threatening:
Will I drop it?
Will I?

§

I needed an empty chalkboard
of a boy, where I could write
my name in large, large letters.

More: a markerboard
where I could write MARY MARY
in forbidden permanent

marker, impossible
to erase, like her sweet face
hovering over your bed

every night.

Tomboy

It was always about power.
You wouldn't find me in skirt scattered
by gale or flurry, fingers fluttering
to hold down wild hems.

I needed you to be able to hear
my heavy approach, storm-like,
my boots stirruped by bullets, clattering
with Spencer's silver sword and skull

earrings, inverted pentacles. *Real men
wear black and silver*, said a t-shirt,
and so did I. God would not command me,
nor opinion, nor the squeals and smirks

of bug-shy girls, batting away
both unwanted bees and wanted boys.
You're not like most girls, a boyfriend
commended me, and I was proud.

§

Years later my ex-husband and I
found a thirteen year-old girl,
punk-spiked bleached hair, chains
and put-on toughness, sobbing

lopsidedly out of the Commons,
silver-plated belt undone, shirt
on backwards. *They stole my music.
I thought they were my friends.*

We coaxed her to hand over her cell
and called her mother, who met us,
asking, *Has she been raped?*

All we could say: *We don't know.*

§

I brought an underweight, awkward friend
to a party once: two beers in, she stumbled
and slurred; three, she went to bed
with a crush. I was disgusted; I didn't think

anyone could get drunk that quickly.
Then the other boys-- my friends--
started going into that room--

I was having a good time.
I didn't want a lot of drama.
How dare she start this argument
between my yin & yang?

A woman who is any kind of woman
would have called someone, taken her home.
But I wasn't any kind of woman, was I?

§

The gutter-punks who hung around
the Commons condemned only one person:
not the thirty year-old man who bought
the booze, or the street kids who stole from her,

but the thirteen year-old girl.
She couldn't handle her alcohol,
they sneered, while an overdue
awareness awakened in me and shouted:

She's thirteen years old!
She's thirteen years old!

§

I, ever rational, handled my alcohol.
I took what I wanted; sovereign,
stoic. I marked my boundary lines.
I was one of the guys.

So why this sign of his intrusion:
a single strand of his hair
woven into the teeth of my zipper?
The hours of the night fogged over.

One Long Black Hair

I woke up the next morning
blinking at my pink canopy
with no recollection

of how I'd gotten home:
had mom picked me up?
what the fuck had I said/done?

It was alarming, so I smudged
it out, easy in plainspoken day,
with its sharp shadows.

Alone with my boyfriend, later,
he unzipped my pants
to find one long, black hair

braided through the blunt
teeth of the zipper--
This is --------- 's.

Said without hesitation, without doubt,
without a question mark of rising sound.
No, peering through my mind's tides--

as when a later boyfriend
swimming, leading me into the deeps,
turned suddenly around

because something large, white and round
was beneath him. Under the murk
it could've been a waterworn

granite chunk, but it also could've been
a flat-faced ray, with its Medusa
moaning-mouth and zombie eyes,

so he swam like the swim-team racer
he once was, pausing only to shout:

Turn back! Turn back!

--so I turned back.
I said, "*But my brother
also has long black hair,*"

and he said, *In your zipper?*
(seriously, entwined in the copper
row, a hair too long, even I knew)

I said, *Yes, of course: we live
in the same house, all my clothes
and his tossed in the same washer,*

same dryer, whirled about--
It was enough. He believed it.
Even I believed it.

Voices

Recently I've thought of him often,
my unloved teenage boyfriend, how

in his small stature our bodies
locked together like puzzle pieces,

how I learned, in some measure,
if not love, then at least pleasure.

It's the voices in the trees I keep
returning to. It was a decently bright

and mild day that faded into a mild night,
crickets, the pilgrim headlights of cars

passing over the bridge above us,
the bridge nestled in the trees.

The trees were thin and bony like us,
wild and scraggly, not the sturdy things

one would prefer for climbing. So naturally
as blue draped itself over the branches,

I did not believe him when he said
there were voices in the trees.

As night spilled around us and filled
the trees with deep nothing, as the traffic's

river dried to a drizzle, he kept insisting
people were in the trees, people laughing

quietly, implausibly, at him. I've kept
a tendency to leap to the aftermath,

to focus on that, the meat of the story:
him growing so angry, pinning and choking me,

how I ran thunking in my boots drunkenly
down the tracks, returning to his house,

and hid under his father's truck. I forget
the uneasy rustle of the trees when talk

fell down between us, and we stared
at the landscape of cracks in the cement

behind the building where we sat,
how he grew increasingly agitated:

Don't you hear that? Don't you hear that?
How it morphed into a large thing from there:

sounds I didn't hear, then voices, then voices
laughing, then at last a whole tribe of tree-dwellers,

a tribe I was in league with, and I had brought
him there, in order that he may be laughed at.

How my denials of the insistent noise
must have turned sinister in his mind,

how as his panic spread over the night
I refused to hear him, and even laughed.

How his nightmares manifested themselves.
How in them he knew he was not loved.

[32]

Becoming Persephone

We'd sprayed gold paint into paper bags
and huffed the fumes. Detached from body,

self a phosphorescent bubble ahover in some
bright-colored world, somewhere askance

from here. My boyfriend passed out.
Sometimes, when one says *love*, she means

A sour drink that tastes better than loneliness
or *the door that leads out of myself.*

§

I'd started young on some ill-trodden
overgrown path, one with *No Trespassing*

and *Beware* and *At Your Own Risk*
sprinkled along the borders like flowers.

Love was so big, right? Yet everyone
claimed they were in it. One day

walking through the halls of Park Junior High
I saw a wild-haired girl with the same smashed glamour

as Courtney Love, wearing a shirt that said,
If I can't find Love, I'll settle for Lust.

The word *love* was in a smarmy, flowery script.
The word *lust* burned with pain. It seared

like something real. I'd found my philosophy.

§

Many miles down my coyote-smitten, wild
tiger lily-ridden path of lust I was walking

into the school cafeteria and saw you. I dropped
all my books. Just like nothing special

it had happened: I'd stumbled onto Love.

§

You sat beside me on the couch and somehow
with few words said we were kissing.

You stopped to say *I love you.* You need to understand
I wouldn't remember this for a year. The golden fumes

plucked us free from chronology, from history.
I said I loved my boyfriend. I will never know why.

§

Next thing you're on the porch swinging your legs,
back to us, pouting, saying *Fuck you* to every entreaty.

I sat in your friend's lap and he said *Do you want
to fuck him?* I said *yes* and at least that was true.

She says she wants to fuck you buddy! he yelled
out to the porch and then I don't know what, it isn't clear,

I was waking up, being jerked about violently,
I didn't know where I was, I realized I was being fucked

so I called out my boyfriend's name. Suddenly a hand
slapped me, covered my mouth, and there you were,

menacing, angry, hair about you like a patch of briars
saying, *Look who is fucking you now, bitch!*

§

I think I realized I loved you one day in your car.
We were all laughing and it was summer, so bright,

sunlight was glazing the windshield in stripes.
Suddenly I felt very blessed so blessed and I knew

this was about being with you.

§

Once a health and nutrition teacher told us
that there is no love like your first love,

that you will grow up and love others and get married
but you'll always remember the first one.

The class bullies laughed and made fun
when he said they were still close friends.

Ye gods it was not meant to be like this.

§

Some days I still fantasize we run into each other
in a bar or Walmart or at the mall and it takes a moment

before we recognize one another. We mist over
that night or we don't mention it at all.

We go out we have drinks we decide on – not fall into--
loving, and with caresses simple and gentle we undo

the night with the gold paint, we make it right somehow,
and it doesn't matter what happens next because then

it is fixed. I am fixed. You are fixed. We are normal
people again, like we should have been all along.

§

Of course this will never happen. All that can happen
is for me to have the courage to finally be

my hearthstone, my guidepost, my goddess Persephone--
holding Spring in one hand, Hell in the other--

Saying, *You were my first love. You raped me.*
Yet, underneath the fury, I still love you.

Poem with Quotes from a Dream Dictionary

To dream that you are showering with someone suggests
there is something you need to come clean about, confess--
but I've confessed all to you, my hate and my love. I've chased
your blue truck into valleys fuzzed with trees & tall weeds,
to catch you in a stomped-dirt driveway & finish our suspended
conversation.

To dream that you are young again indicates
your failed attempts to rectify past mistakes.
Although your teeth are still white & neat in obedient formation,
your eyes like ink acid-droppered into milk, lean waist,
you're not here to take back what you called me:
painted vase, contents unimportant. You're
leaning forward, lips hinging open like devouring gates:
welcome, hellcome home--

To see or pass through a gate
suggests that you are walking through a new phase
of life. I'm chapters and chapters past you now,
so many pages turned, the old ones have gone to dust
& creepervine, yet at sleep-time, you sweet-lime
your silent way into my clean sheets, where quick-breath,
you rise & fall--

To dream about sex refers to merging. You need
to incorporate aspects of your dream partner
into your own character.
Lightning-fist, black hair like a cowl,
like a mourning veil. Like a cloud
heavy-bellied with rage, sagging
to break, your soul slops over the graveyard,
angry at even the dead--

[37]

To dream that you are in a graveyard represents
the discarded aspects of yourself.
Should I find the clouds in myself and water them
with my little red plastic watering can
until they are pregnant with revenge? In another
dream I stabbed you, and threw the knife
into the lake of the mansion we broke into,
that decadent life we grabbed as if
the world owed us everything, were already ours.

To dream that you kill someone
indicates that you are on the verge.
Consider the person. Do you feel any rage?
Goddam yes I do. I was high, motherfucker,
and you put your hand over my mouth,
so they wouldn't hear me scream.
I was your friend, one of the guys, your drinking pal,
you pretty, pretty motherfucker.

To see a lake in your dream signifies your state of mind.
You feel restricted that you can't express
goddam motherfucker goddam. I was seventeen
and you the wrecking ball of the new-built house.
So I stabbed you good; you were smiling.

Alternatively, the lake may provide you with solace.
If the lake is clear and calm, if the lake eats the knife
without so much as a gulp, and its skin never undulates,
then it symbolizes your inner peace.

If in the dream the lake was stolen, the stealing suggests
that you are feeling deprived. The locale is indicative
of your neediness. So we stole a whole mansion,
with a lake & Godfather-staircase & spa
& a bathroom as big & vaulted as a cathedral,
and why but we were seventeen that's why,
seventeen goddam you.

To dream that you are urinating symbolizes
a release of negative or repressed emotions.
When you left the shower with your slender waist
& droplets prisming from your flicked mane,
I squatted and peed down the drain.

To dream of a knife signifies that the stars
are tinsel merely,
when I'd like to take that blade and ting them,
reverberation, reverberation.

To see a blade suggests that you need
to be able to make clear distinctions:
house cat, wharf rat; spa, seventh level of Dante's hell;
hand grenade, warm dinner roll.

To see a grenade
suggests that your suppressed
emotions are about to explode.

LSD

One thing I learned:
time is not linear; it is cyclical.
The past washes over us

again & again. Again
we move room to room
without reason, again

moonlight through car's
rear window pierces stalk-like
in neat lines, only you and I

see it, think it is solid
enough to touch,
our amazed fingers push

through the bands
of bluish light. Starshine
tinkles like wind chimes

and again your cyanide
halo astonishes me,
your back to the window,

again your hand silencing
my mouth, my cunt sore
for days after, my mind

--the ways of the underworld
are perfect, they
must not be questioned--

[40]

my mind pulls thick curtain
to hide it, my mind parts
the curtain inch by inch.

You thought you only broke
the vase of me, temporary
& fixable. You thought

only once did you pluck
my daisy petals one by one:
she loves me, she loves me not

but time swings around
like a truck descending
a mountain, switchbacks

onto itself, returns
to the same view, only
deeper in the valley.

You cannot cut time
like a fishing line,
let the past drift downstream,

hook still in my mouth.
We return again & again
to that shore, predator

& prey. My impalement
still stingingly fresh.
Red bloom still on my face.

Paradox

My friend of the midnight locks,
lock-picker, window-smasher,

builder of small bonfires
in scrubby fields and in me,

I will not forget that it was your hands--
those violent, bloodstained hands--

who pulled my raging boyfriend
from my fragile body when he,

chokehold around my neck, had intent
to kill. I strangle on this-- broken

by both of you as I am. I spit
and spit it out. You did this not once,

not twice, but over so many blurred nights
I cannot count. My friend, my rapist,

without you and your damned hands
I'd never seen my eighteenth year.

The Children of My Rapist

Since I no longer pray,
I tried centering myself in church, my mom
tugging on my sleeve when it was time to stand.

Entranced, I checked in: my sacral chakra
seemed to have disappeared, a dumb anchor
in a chilly sea; the protection I'd built

around my heart chakra turned out
to be a nest, and all the eggs were cracking.
It was a nest, and the cracked eggs were screaming.

A tennis ball blocked off my throat chakra,
initiating a scratchy pain
that shot straight to my right inner ear.

The ear he hit me in, I thought, and,
There's still something I need to say.

§

I become a movie internet sleuth.
You do it like this: in your pajamas
you sit cross-legged on your half-made bed

and snoop using google, facebook, instagram.
I find his reputation is 86% positive. I know
his wife's name, his baby-mama's name,

the names of his sons. I facebook them:
faces smooth and taut as waxed apples.
Pop bands, sports: they are not at all like him.

[43]

Who has prayed their names under crescent moon
and stars so bright they seem on uppers,
to deities and demons known and unknown?

Will those prayers be answered?

§

I find no extant photos of him, instead,
a possible relative of indeterminate age,
whose brows and cheeks are swollen

with the waters of indifference, of years.
The photo album in my head has suffered
bright empty rings of sun exposure,

fretted edges, circular gray stains
that may be tears. The photos have been enlarged
by importance until the pores of his skin

could be snaps from the rover on Mars.
They have been shrunk so small for transmission
over distance, they're hardly more

than the endless blips of binary code
we all swim in, numerous as grains of sand,
numberless as the stars. Amen.

§

It falls out like it falls out, always:
the boy is made of water. What charges
are made cannot stick, float away

like discarded soda bottles to litter
a tropical cove. What charges
aren't made leave him

with a reputation of good, by 86%.
He loves and leaves and raises nice boys.
In a good year he makes more than the girl,

in a bad year, the same. The girl's
aura changes color like a mood ring
held under hot water, then cold.

She falls through decades
in the haphazard fashion such girls do,
then finds a tennis ball in her throat chakra

the Sunday after Easter,
and even though she's a writer,
she doesn't know what to do.

§

I should save a word for those hatchlings,
my only young. When they cry too shrill
I soak their soft feathers in red wine

until, pouting, they settle down.
Sometimes, late at night, I feed them
shreds of flesh plucked from *Forensic Files*.

Yuck, yuck, whines my mother
from the far end of the couch. Born from violence,
the little hatchlings fill their gaping mouths.

The Light Chain

How we filled the room
with ourselves until it was a pool
sloshing with mockery and howls.
We were loud and brash and laughed a lot.

After we dimmed a bit, at last,
an irritating buzz tapped
out of the background into focus,
punctuated with fleshy thumps,

and looking up, we saw eight
fat flies bumper-carring the bulb,
circling it as we would a twigfire,
raging, drunk with brightness.

When you took off your shoe,
and stood on your chair,
you still had to leap
to smash them.

We laughed, of course,
until one boy said, you're making a mess,
and we all agreed you should come down.

But you refused, swearing;
slavering in a Bacchic trance,
you crushed the last of the little beasts.

After this it rolls out, film from a tin:
you beating that boy who never wronged you:
three fast flash jabs, glare of your teeth,

[46]

him falling in a roar that either came
from your mouth or echoed out
from my own;

you slapping your girlfriend to the graveyard's
ground for pissing on a grave,
and finally, of course, turning on me.

I pull the light chain on this night.
The blood lingers on the lambent white.

Crushed

Darling, after all these years, I still don't know
what love is. We were drunk in an aging alcoholic's

trailer. He was a pitiful, lopsided-faced muppet
of a man, and we used him: full reign over his home

for the price of a few cans of Pabst Blue Ribbon.
We kept the better stuff for ourselves. Explaining

teenage boyhood to me, you made love to smoke-stained
curtains, shouting, *Woo! Woo! A guy'd do*

anything, even this curtain! We celebrated our night's lease
on the old man's home by jumping up and down

on the couch, crashing to the ground headbanging,
while he, smiling, ambled out for a quieter room.

Later, spent by silliness, you sat on the floor
close by me, and slid sideways across the burn-

riddled couch in the world's fakest faint. Twenty-five
years on I wake from sleep with one late tear

creeping across my cheek for that moment when
your head rested on my jean-clad leg so gently.

II

You drift between earth and death
which seem, finally,
strangely alike.

--Louise Glück
from "Persephone the Wanderer"

Pierced Septum

after the film *Audrie & Daisy*

After she was raped, the girl's clothes
turned dark and loose. Her blonde hair

bled black, which she couldn't cover fully
with her charcoal cap. Even this

wasn't sufficient for the nighttime
pouring out of her: it tainted her bedroom,

the pictures she scrawled in a sketchpad,
even the air around her as she breathed.

She was a black hole in reverse,
an infinite density of darkness spilling

outwards, outwards. I don't know
what happened to her little giggles,

light as butterflies. She grew spiky
piercings from her once gentle face.

The boys went on with their lives,
they graduated, they're going to college,

they're making something of themselves.
The girl? The sheriff shrugs. And smiles.

She has a septum piercing, a crescent
with two sharp spikes pointing down.

It says, *Don't even try to kiss me.*
It's an ugliness only the right man

will be able to see around.

Set Apart

In the years after, I stopped perming and dying my hair. My taut red ringlets loosened, fell frayed and golden-brown. I stopped applying make-up; my pale face shone.

I heard Paul say, *When we were in the realm of the flesh, the sinful passions were at work in us, so that we bore fruit for death,*

and I was glad to hear that being in the body, being one with the body, was death. I wore loose clothes that hid my breasts and thighs.

I felt the real, essential me was floating above my body. *I had died to what once bound me.* Sometimes I couldn't feel my arms and legs. I was *serving in the new way of the Spirit.*

Holy in the Greek is *hagios*, meaning *set apart.*

I was grateful that I had become holy. My emotions etherized-- not euthanized but etherized-- were sublime.

Only when a group of boys shouted from their car, *Cut your hair, you freak!* did I realize I had dispensed with my gender.

§

I swear it was new, and sweet, like being *born again*, as innocent as a child, as a young child, a toddler.

The old me had died! The new me did not then consider how this sundering, this plundering of me to remove myself, to quit the body that had been raped,

placed me, *pure spirit*, far from the defiled body, safe from her, detached.

[52]

Trailer Park

In my early twenties, I took my love
like a punishment, like a sour medicine

so foul I'd need a few gulps to drain
the little plastic dosing cup.

My love was reckless: he spent
our grocery money on crack,

drained the account, wrote bad checks,
drove home drunk on the backroads

and woke in the car, crookedly-
parked in the yard. He was cruel:

he told me he could easily find
other lovers, better looking ones,

girls who shaved their pussies,
had tan lines, got manicures,

wore sexy underwear. I was
a bad cook, a sloppy homemaker.

Once he stabbed a fork into the clean
finish of the kitchen table, leaving a gouge,

and I don't even remember why.
But I did have a parted-grass path

that led to a wildflower spangled meadow.
In the corner of the meadow, a drive camper

slowly teetered toward the earth, weeds poking
from its windows. A flock of turkeys

drowsed lazy-eyed in the field as if
it were their living room; at the sight of me

they'd trot into the forest with one collective
jabbering gobble that made me giggle,

bobbing their heads, their wattles jiggling.
I had a forgotten footpath that led to a quiet,

clear stream. It liked to mutter softly
as the wind worried the leaves.

Even then I had the kind world to commune with,
before I returned home to be thrown

for my many and obvious shortcomings
against the trailer's thin, shuddering wall.

Below Zero, with Wind Chill

The ever-moving ocean freezes mid-motion:
        ripples dollop in peaks,
                ridges burst into crests, then stop.

(I'm the sort of woman who takes a long walk
        in weather below zero, crosses a park alone
                in the dark of the Boston suburbs.

I'll walk home from a bar
        at 3 a.m. with only my fast little feet
                to save me. Women like me deserve what they get.)

The water farther down the wharf had slopped
        against the rocks, then stuck. Round pimples raised
                then popped into toothily jagged crowns, caught

(you got me good, and so my womb,
        rocked and lured to lunacy by the tidal moon,
                hardened into sea-glass, faceless and pristine)

caught outstretched like fingers of praise, water slowed to the motions
        of maple, whose leaping toward the well-loved sun
                is so torpid our tricked eyes see permanence,

(So I started reaching for Heaven, for that purified form
        when the body drops away like a pod from a seed
                leaving only the real, the untouched, stone, me)

chilled and sealed under glass, a display. I could see a single seaweed
        standing still as a tree. Then the wind blue-hued the rocks
                in a great confusion, what with the sky on the ground

(and the body woke up as if from a coma, limbs unused and foreign,
      and the sky on the ground. Heaven in the forest. Lunatic
           again and fighting it, calling my heavings and surges evil.)

while a siren hooted from the salted streets of my town, and the geese
      spun as music-box harlequins to face it and mimicked
           the sound. The gulls by the lighthouse yellowed in day's end

(How I policed me. How I cuffed my own hands and bound my own feet,
      shuffling about in my orange shame, sitting myself down in my cage.
           Scratching prayers into the cell wall, which my own nature answered)

and I peered out past them where the water went from white to navy blue,
      as if the night were trapped in it. The night is trapped in me too, and the stars,
           so small in its vastness, so weak, and so silent.

Sailing Through Fog

Yes, I said, zipping my jacket,
pulling my hood down over my eyes,
peering out of that shaded place
into undifferentiated white.

Yes, let's go sailing. Let's thrust
our fragile mortal bodies
onto moody harbor waters
while blindfolded by fog.

Once on the waves, a crowd of ghosts.
Masts and hulls rearing like startled
steeds of the Apocalypse; the shore
a suggestion, a guess, or a wish.

Now that I'm stuck on this tiny wedge of wood
with him, now there's no bathroom to excuse
myself to, now that I can't point at my watch,
nod sadly, and walk home, now

he wants to debate proving or disproving
Holy Writ. I decline and say it's not
the point, the power of the story is the point.
But it's time to tack, and *grab those lines,*

no silly, loosen up, not so tight. The ropes
slip over my palms roughly, the sail knocks
and shimmies and finally fills out. He tacks;
he's talking about the anchor's power,

bottom-dredging truth, a safe mooring.
He says, *Steer away from the lighthouse;*
let's see how high we can point. The jib
bellies and the ghosts gather close.

He says there's no absolute truth.
The boat sways in a wake, and I wonder
is it safe out here, away from the dock,
choked by fog? The titanic ferry

could bear down on us, as blind to us
as we are to it, a thunderhead
could form and we'd not see it:
waves like trees leaning over our sail-tent.

A cormorant dives sleekly, leaving
only the smallest wrinkle. It will part
the dim ocean heart so long, we won't,
in this fog, chance to see it surface,

but water is its home. We're land beasts:
lumbering, fragile. He says fear
is the issue, it's why we believe beyond reason.
The fog thickens, and with it comes the cold.

Nothing But the Blood

In church as a child, where the Pledged pews
forced spines into unpleasant uprightness,
(by sermon's end I'd be drooping carpetward,)

he'd sing: round little man, lumpy as a dog's bed,
crooning coffeehouse acoustic, eyes closed
or unfocused off to the left somewhere, gone,

then he'd return, stooping a bit under applause,
plump cheeks tucked upward in embarrassment,
while the pastor thanked him for his message in song.

He'd remember my name and always greet me.
He'd stand at service's end to deliver the news: men's
brunch on Saturday, and remember the family

of long-on-the-prayer-list-name. I don't know
what mad dog grabbed his washed-whiter-than-snow
in its teeth and shook and shook.

It looked real, didn't it, under the definite,
decorated lamps, in such direct light,
Sunday morning, Sunday evening, Wednesday night?

It was real. Every cup of Welch's grape juice,
solemnly swallowed. Head bowed, sweat
glistening at the edge of receding hair line.

This too is real: the singer's mug shot
in the Sunday news, the story of his secret sin.
Smudged from dew, left

under my parents' mailbox. Real:
the empty pew, the backlit blue baptism-tank.
He molested a child. There it is, in type:

how the Band-Aid of grace did nothing
for him, even less for his victim; it's peeled off
and the wound won't scab, just bleeds.

§

The Orthodox Presbyterians believe
that while some of us are predestined

to be saved, others are predestined
to be damned.

§

So I too bleed from my wound: the dream
wherein you, mid-sentence, lean in
to kiss me, and I lean too, and I fall

headfirst into bewilderment and awe.
What mad dog is this, opening
Tiamat's maw to savage our fences,

allowing such a collision? a god
to be worshiped? a devil to be choked?
The singing man said:

I have always been attracted
to young children.

He is not twisted, to be untwisted;
he is not dirty, to be cleaned;
he is an arrow shot from birth

that cannot, by a million tiny cups
tipped in reverence, in belief,
be knocked astray. So are we all

shot into our unfathomable distances:
he to wound a child; I to wound you;
you to wound me.

Tuesday is Trash Day

The skittering sunlight is a honey-lemon hue,
replacing winter's glare, washed-out and sullen.
I walk in sneakers instead of boots, without
gloves or a cap, a scarf even.

Shine and shadow make a lattice of lines
under the still-barren trees. I need
a tidy mind like that. I'd like
a well-tended row of peonies, please--

But it's trash day and the barrels
are out, windblown on the walkway,
overturned, stench lingering.
I weave down the street to avoid them.

A sparrow sings merrily atop
a discarded computer monitor.
A single new green leaf has fallen.
I dodge dogs and at the Common

veer to the blue of the cove, where
polished water sapphires, but the shore
is a mess from yesterday's rain
and swollen tide. Like love is a mess

I tell myself, like family is, like
the mind. Nasty wads of paper
and plastic bags wetly wrap
god knows what. I walk a wide arc

around it in the sodden grass,
not wanting to look. Like love
is a mess, like I try not to remember
the dream where a friend I thought

was a friend leaned forward mid-
sentence and kissed me, gently,
timidly. After, we stepped back,
regarded one another with abashed alarm.

I walk a wide arc around. Ahead,
budding birch trees are frizzled
with crimson agitation. And what
is budding in me, flaring redly?

[62]

What green thing will unfurl and flatten
whether or not I stay here to watch?
What has washed up on my shore?
Who will drag the dirty barrels away?

Hymn to Aphrodite

My basement is flooded,
O Lady of the Waters,
the foundation eroded.
Rowboats skim in and out of windows;
their captains are calling,
The house is falling,
the house is falling.

Now you dredge the depths
and lift up shipwrecks to the sun
and lift up many-tentacled beasts
with light-dead eyes
and lay them on our beach.
See them, you say, *see them!*

You twirl your dark and terrible skirts,
and laughing, dance your hurricane inland,
exhaling and peeling back roofs.
Docks are untoothed board by board,
Lady Born of the Sea,
where we stood and thought
you sun-smitten and lovely,
lovely and harmless.

Let the Current Take You

At the edge of the beach a small river meets the ocean. I should have
been a pair of ragged claws. Children are floating down it. Scuttling
across the floors. Some of them have rafts, some don't.
Of silent seas. I'm guessing the relationship of the mind to the body
is not that of a child on a raft floating out to sea, squealing merrily. A
raftless brother and sister float by me. The boy is moving sluggishly.
I step in and sink in soft sand. The current pulls on my legs like wind
pulling a long skirt, trying to make me trip. This is similar to when I
step in desire. A comedian once said that to a man falling in love is
like stepping in dog shit. The man looks at his shoe. *Shit*, he says, but
he means *Love.* The sister yells, *Ball! Ball!* and the brother responds,
Ball! It's like the secret language shared by twins. It's like Aramaic to
me; I don't understand it but I'm sure it's holy. Like a poked pillbug
the brother tucks himself into a ball. The relationship of the body to
the mind should not be that of a poked pillbug, and the finger that
pokes it, scolds it. The current sweeps the boy past me quickly. I want
to be as innocent as a child, so I step farther out into the current.

Ball, I whisper to myself and curl up. Instantly I'm jetted past the old
couple who were trying the waters beside me. As I'm carried along as
swiftly as an empty Coke bottle they seem to reconsider. I'm not an
empty Coke bottle. I'm trying to erase my adulthood, all those long
years of mistakes. A gradual disaster, John Banville called it. The man
who stepped in Love shows his shoe to his friends. *Get it off! Get it
off!* he cries. Suddenly I stop; I'm stuck on a sandbar. I am too big for
innocence, I think. The man's friends laugh at him. *I'm not touching
that,* they say, *You're on your own.* The relationship of the mind to the
body could be like that of quarters and the pockets filled by them,
weighing them down. It's like I'm going to the damn laundromat
here. I stand and wade again. Again I sink step by step. Again I say,
Ball, a magic word, a word that makes this work for me, so large and
gangly. I'm off again and I see the beach recede, the mothers and
babies grow smaller and smaller.

[65]

Perhaps the body is like a baby that laughs at the ocean's edge, smacking tiny fists into the shallow water. Perhaps the mind is his mother, making sure he doesn't crawl into the waves. *Ball! Ball!* I giggle, glad it's working, but then I turn my head to see I'm cruising toward sharp-looking rocks. I don't know what happened to the man with Love on his shoe. I don't know where the old couple have gone. Perhaps the mind is like my arms and legs, now extended, now working hard against the once-enchanting current. I am not a ball and if I hit those rocks, I won't bounce. Perhaps the body is like the Coke bottle, carried away in the current, lost, lost.

A Literal Reading of an April Pond

On the new-thawed spring pond
gulls gather to paddle in a cloister
of white on the gray not-yet
summer water. I often wonder

how their flat orange feet
can stand the quaking cold.
The ice has broken, the upper pond
flows in torrents into the lower,

louder than normal, roiling whitely.
One would say *raging* but water
has no heart. The gulls are lifting
their weathered white bellies

with flightless flapping, backs
arched as if dreaming of lift,
necks outstretched toward the passage
into the harbor. But they don't go,

as if anchored by cold, they give
and sink back in. This is beauty to me:
the yearning reach, the give and fall,
because I am hoping to leave this path

between the ponds that goes nowhere,
this stuck place between the lower and upper
waters, I am reaching with open-sea hope
for a sky that the cold won't let me own,

I am falling back into the freezing.
The ice has thawed but the air stays chilly.
The water and sky are winter-gray.
The falls resound with purposed motion.

I want to add: May is close, the winds will warm!
The gulls will gather their strength and take
to sky, and sky will blush blue over June ocean,
and these things are signs that all I wish will happen.

Yet I know I have ensouled the gulls
with yearning and sea-hope, while their brains
are gray slates like the pond's face.
I know the water-rush is devoid of intent.

Although spring comes it comes
without a promise for my station in life,
my wishes for forward movement,
for life as open as the wide wide sea.

I am aware I am a poet feeding
my meaning into the mindless scene:
gulls and water and winter wind being,
and no god speaking through these to me.

Fog on Derby Wharf

The heat was dense and buttery
but the fog lay cool about the bay.
The fog like shutters sealing

Salem into itself, ocean beyond
sight, boats dissolving ghostlike
into the oncoming nothing.

The powerplant is gone, *man,*
said one of the Pokemon players
seated on the rocks of the wharf,

who looked up, with laugh and shrug,
just long enough to note the encroachment
before falling again into his screen.

Isolated as if the wharf were empty,
I watch the fog eat the water,
ripple by ripple, ease

toward all of us gently, breathing cool,
breathing rest. All the shores vanish;
the way back is lost.

We seem to occupy the one last stretch
of sunlight, we-- the players and I--
are left untouched by the wet hands

of the land-fallen cloud. Why not us?
I ask myself, why so clear in this circle
of bright? But then I know it:

we're in it. If we'd move our circle
would move with us. You never think
you're in the fog; you're always safe

in your little capsule of knowing.
You walk toward and toward it.
It seems to part to let you pass.

Threshold

A day as clear as the rim of a wave
where it rolls over stone, broken glass
in browns, milky whites, greens.
A sepia shard is stuck in sand,
piercing edge up; I carefully pluck it
from the shining shallows.

The thresholds of the waves are silk.
The glaze on them, pearl and honest.
A man looses his red husky
who wades in, tongue lolling,
swims out just over her head,
then back, methodically.

I think of how a man goes to his grave:
he wears his wedding band.
A photo of him,
smiling in his Sunday suit,
is displayed by the casket.

The lid of his casket is adorned
with a painting of the buck
he searched out and shot:
here it leaps a restive creek,
strength still in its dainty legs.

A military flag is folded
and handed to his weeping wife.
Twenty-one blank shots are fired
into the silence of the churchyard.

The dog swims out and back.
I like to think she enjoys it,
but her jowls are slack,
her eyes flat and eerie.

When I plunge into the cool cove
I swim until the voices on the shore
are lost. Only the sound
of the water I stir, gurgling
around my arms as I hover.
I could swim as far as sight
and not tire. My lover
walks to the water's edge, waves.

I wave back.
The dog is tied in the shade.
Children stand on rocks.

The meaning drains from the scene
like water from an office cooler,

and you'd think the color would drain, too.
You'd think the world would be
an Ansel Adams print:
precise, so many shades of gray
inside this certain frame.

Instead color fills
the children, the dog, her owner
and the bench on which he sits,
my lover sighing, hands on hips;

the rocks and water and sand,
and reddening corpses
of washed-up crabs,
and trees and vines,
houses and sky

all fill up with vibrant hues
as water is poured in a glass.
The glass is brittle and will break,
will break, one day soon.

I swim for the shore swiftly
until arms and legs burn and ache
and the fire I feel is life.
I emerge, dripping.

I embrace my lover,
who giggles when my cold breasts
touch his sun-warmed chest.
We stand on the shore in the sun.

We hold on, tight.

III

But when the earth starts blossoming with fragrant flowers of
springtime,

flowers of every sort, then it is that you must come up from the misty
realms of darkness,

once again, a great thing of wonder to gods and mortal humans alike.

--from "Homeric Hymn to Demeter"
trans. by Gregory Nagy

Turn Lane

The first few times I drove a car
I remember this feeling of nakedness

or displacement: as if I were walking
down the center of the road,

or standing over the arrow painted on the turn lane,
waiting for the light to change,

or stepping out into the street
in front of a moving car. They said:

the car will feel like an extension of you,
and it did. What I could not accept

was that I had a place in this flow
of headlights and taillights. No,

I would always be a child standing
on the edges, remembering to look both ways,

slipping across a street on quiet feet
quickly. If I could make that shift inside myself

now, that moment of acceptance, of saying:
yes, I belong on this road between the yellow

and white lines, beside this pick-up truck
also waiting for the green light, I belong

as much as anyone. If I could again reach out
of my frail body and become those four doors

and those four wheels on this, my road. If
I could make that shift again. Right now.

Divorcing Plato

Each day, I strive to shuck the sickness you infected me with:

I eat the rotini with the homemade marinara and I drink the better
bottle of Chianti.

When I see a lovely body I say, *what a lovely body*, without shame, and I
look and look because this is the gift and there is no better form.

I walk around the lake in the frank January sun and am astonished by
the storm-shattered trunks of trees jutting from the sooty snow, and I
don't say, how far you fall, broken tree, from the ideal tree somewhere
in the sky.

I loose the dark horse and let him run through the mud if he wants.
You're wrong; he's really a fine horse; oh the pollen-dazzled fields
he finds, the mouthfuls of wildflowers. The white horse now trots
beside him companionably. They no longer fight and struggle; they've
become close as kin.

I love the warm smooth body beside me in bed. The self that wants
dark chocolate and the self that loves the poem are the same self.
When I love the poem I don't love only the thought behind and
through and above it, spanning over it like a great arching bridge,

but I love the syllables and how they walk and dance through the
mouth, over the tongue, and how they enter the ear like music, and
how the limbs may tremble a little with the rhythm.

I'm my writing hands, and my lips kissing the skin of my beloved, and
my love is completed, not soiled, by my hips and his hips together in
the consuming and humid dark.

This body is not a coffin.

Poem With a Stolen Line

My wolf, how long you were fangs to me,
saliva-spangled, quivering oblivion lip, mouth's pink gate.
How long hungry throat. My life

in your gullet. Your yellowed claws
like syringes for blood. You could do nothing
besides belly in dirt, in leaves,

crouching with a snarl, cornered.
I did not want your copper-scented nights.
I did not want your knife-edge stars.

My wolf, I have your four long legs
but I have not learned to run. My wolf,
some scents are missing, in the tapestry

they weave they have left holes,
the colors gone awry, the scene told
indecipherable. Figures gesture

toward empty space. My wolf,
your appetites rumble within my abdomen,
and one day desire will not be

a form of wickedness. Draw near,
my wolf, draw near. My hand
reaches for your pine-prickled coat,

you are stomach of my stomach, we are pack-mates,
we are one bounding hunger in darkness,
we are one set of salt-white teeth.

At the Magick Shop

The customer at the counter--
a well-dressed businessman
of a fluttery, nervous disposition--
is asking the clerk for a spell
to bind a woman's affection to him.

What you're going to do,
the eyebrow-pierced clerk says
matter-of-factly, *is buy
a love or lust candle,
either one will work...*

What an idea! I think.
*To imagine love and lust
are the same thing!*

Two-Bird Hymn to Ishtar

The cormorant perches on a rock in the shallows,
a chip of coal in unchecked bright, a tear-drop
of midnight in midday, black as the shadow
under the sofa, where anything could be hidden.

Not fifteen feet off, the egret tiptoes in weedbed,
shock of laundry-white, cleaner than my best socks,
white as sanitized countertop, where not even
invisible evil resides.

And at last these two clear a path to you,
unfathomable lady, who is and is not,
who is wicked and blameless, and to what
you signify

with two owls by your owl-clawed feet.
What were you holding, bare-breasted mystery,
smiling so emptily? Queen of cormorant

who dives beneath murk and seaweed,
who scours the bottoms, unsettles the mud,
black-winged, darkness-breasted, touched
by the wet of it, soaked, shining,

and egret who stands above on stick-leg stilts,
also shining, unsullied, sun-spangled, who dips beak
daintily and keeps every feather dry.

Yours the mirror of the lake-face, and who
can bear it. Yours the shattering of becauses,
the unraveling of story-lines, the lies

told to keep feathers dry. Yours the long dive
into the dark, the muddied beak,
the stirring of dirty depths, what soaks

and takes so long to dry. Yours also
the strength of the legs that lift
above all saturations, that bear

with dignity the clean bright neck.
Shy in the shallows, she hides from me,
shimmies her neck snake-like, finds
me wanting, steps into sky, glides

to far shore. Cormorant stays close by.
Such is the season you have decreed for me,
O double-natured lady.

Birth of Aphrodite

Aphrodite was formed in the depths of the seas.
Let me tell you what this means: suppose

it is August and you in your sweaty underwear
and billowy sundress, after a few

honey-wheat ales, note a man singing
to the room, and he's not the most handsome man,

but his slender large nose matches his
demanding chin, and his voice is a candle.

You love the way his hands glide over
the neck of his guitar. Your body

sighs and births a little neon fish
in your ocean. You don't notice.

Later, you talk to him. You like the haughty
way he holds his frame, feet apart

and resting back on them, aloof,
the shades half-drawn on his eyes, his smirk.

Now there's a little school down there,
surging first this way then that.

When he parts his lips that you rather like
a red tulip blooms from them,

with its startling yellow cup and dusty
black stamens. Within the seas

of your subconscious mind
where dragons dwell and octopi

bigger and stranger than a star gone nova,
he is pieced together, this secret work

all unknown to you: your jailer's cuffs,
your twice-tied knot, your candy heart

too beautiful to eat, too delicious to waste.
Up from the sea the Nereids carry him,

bedewed with your own waters.
Here, they declare, *we give you*

Smasher of Paradigms, the strong-fisted,
he who will kill you so that you will be

reborn, and he is worth any martyrdom.
Now what will you do?

I'll Be Your Little Reaper, When You Die a Little Death

I want to see your face fold and unfold in a pleasure so bad you thrust
your chin forward to show the tiny tombstones of your bottom teeth,
lined neatly in a row.

Once I heard you make a sound so small, it didn't fit your body. I want
to play your body until you make a fluteful of such noises,

twittering like a yellow finch. I want to be the reason your chest
muscles clench, the reason why you hold in your paunch, then forget
and let it go.

Then may my belly be the bowl you spill into

when you've forgotten reason and blame and a flame roars over your
brain, a clean burn.

I want to watch you roll and squirm trying to find the place most in,
most buried.

May my lips be the dam's lock, loosed; may my throat be the gully that
gathers your rivers.

You didn't think I'd do that, so now you laugh, a giggle born in the cage
of your hips that erupts up through your lungs so quick

you're embarrassed, because it's not funny, there's nothing rude or
shrewd with irony,

but you spasm with it, you've walked through the mausoleum gates
and now you're on the other side, blinded and astonished in the sun.

Jazz Birds

At the Salem Jazz & Soul Festival
cormorants were sunning on a rowboat just
offshore, wings outstretched,

at least seven repetitions of the signal
Gotham sends in times of trouble.
Each bird had its head turned

to stare at the stage. *Look!*
said my lover, pointing, *Jazz birds!*
And so they've been.

I'd like to say there's some
mystic meaning to this appellation:
how the bird always sits so low

in shifting blue-black diamonds
of ocean is how we sink down
in the ocean of sound. When

the music takes you under
and you forget where you are,
your ears take over for your eyes

and you hear your way over
the shifting landscape of melody,
like a landscape in a dream.

Bass for the dip down, and then
the jazz bird goes nosing through
the pulpy bulbs of swaying seaweed,

as we fall face first into the
frightening fleshy lumps of our
ignored selves, when we fall

through sound, with bliss & fear
we drown. The jazz bird likes
to get down. The bird knows

that underneath the street clothes
of day-to-day surface shine
we will find the food

to sustain us. Jazz birds
come up, too, up through
saxophone's airy reachings,

to surface in the bright sun.
To sit on the lip of a rowboat
and dry out what's needed

for flight. The birds stare
at the stage, the boat rolls
in a wake, and they nod,

All right, all right, all right.

Notes

"Poem with Quotes from a Dream Dictionary"

Some of the dream symbol interpretations are taken directly from or paraphrased from the website dreammoods.com. Others are of my own invention.

"LSD"

The lines below are paraphrased from *Inanna: Queen and Heaven and Earth* translated by Diane Wolkstein and Samuel Noah Kramer.

--the ways of the underworld
are perfect, they
must not be questioned--

"Set Apart"

The first three sections in italics are paraphrases of Romans 7:5- 7:6.

"Let the Current Take You"

"I should have been a pair of ragged claws/ scuttling across the floors of silent seas" is taken from "The Love Song of J. Alfred Prufrock" by T.S. Eliot.

"Poem with a Stolen Line"

"One day desire will not be a form of wickedness" is a line taken from Terrance Hayes' poem "Shakur."

"Two-Bird Hymn to Ishtar"

The Sumerian goddess Ishtar is seen, among other things, as a goddess of opposites.

Mary Ann Honaker is the author of *It Will Happen Like This* (YesNo Press, 2015). Her work has appeared in *2 Bridges, Drunk Monkeys, Euphony, Juked, Little Patuxent Review, Off the Coast, Van Gogh's Ear*, and elsewhere. Her work has been nominated for a Pushcart prize. Mary Ann holds an MFA in creative writing from Lesley University. She currently lives in Beckley, West Virginia, but considers Salem, Massachusetts, where she lived for many years, her second home.

Thanks to Robert Canipe and Tim Peeler at Third Lung Press for taking on this work. Many thanks to the Salem Writers Group of Salem, MA, led by J.D. Scrimgeour, whose advice changed my writing for the better. Hearty thanks to my mentors at Lesley University's Creative Writing Program: Sharon Bryan, Erin Belieu, and Joan Houlihan, and to the former head of that program, Steven Cramer. Thanks to Eileen Cleary and Chris Lamay-West for their comments and advice on earlier versions of this manuscript. Thanks to my parents, Jim and Frankie Honaker, whose unfailing love has always given me a safe harbor in any storm. Also, thanks to Aepril Schaile, whose wisdom as a spiritual leader carried me through a dark time and helped shape many poems in this book. Thank you to every person who has encouraged me to keep writing, You've all midwifed this book into being.

Awards Earned

Third place in long poetry category, West Virginia Writers 2018.

Nominated for Pushcart Prize, 2018, Night Music Journal.

Second place in poetry chapbook category, West Virginia Writers 2019.

Second place, The Orchard Street Press Poetry Contest 2019.

Finalist, The Orchard Street Press Poetry Contest 2019.

Finalist for the Christopher Smart Prize 2019, Eyewear Editions.

This book has been printed in Garamond Premiere Pro using Display and *Italic Display.* The font was designed by Robert Slimbach for Adobe Fonts when he visited the Plantin-Moretus Museum in Antwerp, Belgium, to study their collection of Claude Garamond's metal punches and type designs. Garamond, a French punch cutter, produced a refined array of book types in the mid-1500s that combined an unprecedented degree of balance and elegance,and stand as a pinnacle of beauty and practicality in type founding. While fine-tuning Adobe Garamond (released in 1989) as a useful design suited to modern publishing, Slimbach started planning an entirely new interpretation of Garamond's designs based on the large range of unique sizes he had seen at the Plantin-Moretus, and on the comparable italics cut by Robert Granjon, Garamond's contemporary. By modeling Garamond Premier Pro on these hand-cut type sizes, Slimbach has retained the varied optical size characteristics and freshness of the original designs, while creating a practical 21st-century type family. Garamond Premier Pro contains an extensive glyph complement, including central European, Cyrillic and Greek characters, and is offered in five weights ranging from light to bold.

About the Publisher

Third Lung Press is an independent publisher that delivers books to readers who otherwise may never have had the opportunity to read them.

Started in 1988 by poet Tim Peeler, it's first issue was a journal created as a writing contest to raise money for OXFAM, a global organization working to end the injustice of poverty and helping people build better futures for themselves, hold the powerful accountable, and save lives in disasters.

Third Lung Press published 32 issues of its saddle-stitched namesake journal and several chapbooks. It published its last issue in 2003.

The press was resurrected in 2017 by Peeler and Robert Canipe to publish Terry Barr's *Don't Date Baptists and Other Warnings from my Alabama Mother* when the book was orphaned by another publisher.

Following it in 2018 was yet another orphaned book from the same publisher, a memoir from Sandra Worsham, *Going To Wings,* that proved to be a bestseller on Amazon.com and in bookstores due to Worsham's relentless touring and reading schedule.

Since then, Third Lung Press has published an additional book by Barr and Worsham, a book of poems by Worthy Evans (*Cold War*), three detective novels by Michael Poovey (The *Inspector October Series*), a thriller by April Rice (*Sacrifices*), and poetry from Beverly C. Finney (*Bearing Witness*).

Third Lung Press is named after the sensation a marathon runner gets when he or she feels like finishing the race is impossible. The runner taps into his or her "third lung" for that extra bit to complete the task.

This is the way of art as well.

Third Lung Press is proud to present to you the work of its newest family member, Mary Ann Honaker, whose heartfelt and raw compositions speak loudly to a world perhaps ready to learn from them.

Thank you for your support.

Made in the
USA
Lexington, KY